ISBN 1-84135-289-6

Copyright © 1994 Award Publications Limited
This edition first published 2004

Published by Award Publications Limited,
27 Longford Street, London NW1 3DZ

Printed in Malaysia

MAGICAL TALES

by Linda Jennings
adapted by Jackie Andrews
Illustrated by Val Biro

AWARD PUBLICATIONS LIMITED

CONTENTS

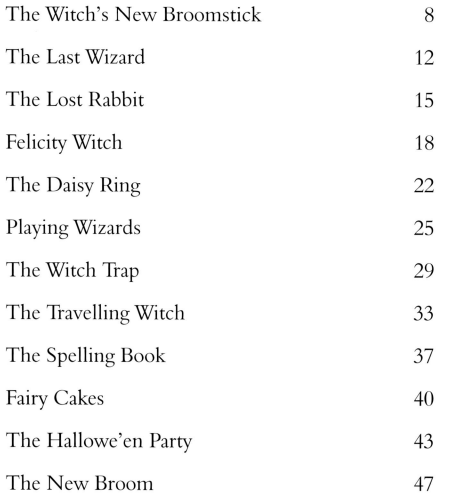

The Witch's New Broomstick   8

The Last Wizard   12

The Lost Rabbit   15

Felicity Witch   18

The Daisy Ring   22

Playing Wizards   25

The Witch Trap   29

The Travelling Witch   33

The Spelling Book   37

Fairy Cakes   40

The Hallowe'en Party   43

The New Broom   47

Nat's Magic Seedling 50

The Broomstick Race 53

The Magic Bicycle 56

The Monster Under the Pavement 59

The Magic Stone 63

Cat on a Broomstick 66

Dragon Fire 69

The Little Yellow Goblin 73

The Monster in the Pool 76

All That Glitters 80

Not Quite a Dragon 83

Witch Twinkletoes 87

The Witch at the Bottom of the Lane 90

THE WITCH'S NEW BROOMSTICK

Witch Nightshade was flying over Hightop Wood one night when the twigs of her old broomstick suddenly fell apart. Fortunately, she was able to land safely.

But there was a problem. How was a witch supposed to get about without a broomstick?

"Bother," she said. "I shall have to buy a new one."

The very next day Witch Nightshade marched into a hardware shop in town, to find herself a new broomstick.

"A broomstick?" said the shop assistant, shaking his head. "There's not much demand for those nowadays."

"But I'm demanding one," said Witch Nightshade.

"That's as may be," said the shop assistant. "But I don't have any."

"Well, what am I to do?" wailed the witch. "I must have a broom! What do people use instead, then?"

"Vacuum cleaners."

"Really?" said Witch Nightshade, who had never seen one. "Perhaps I'd better take a look."

The man looked doubtfully at the witch. She was not the tidiest of people, and really didn't look as if she had two pennies to rub together, let alone enough money to afford a vacuum cleaner. But he took her through into the showroom and showed her the latest models.

"Oooh," said Witch Nightshade. "They're lovely!" She went over to a streamlined green and beige vacuum cleaner and lovingly stroked it. She was thinking what a sensation she would cause in the coven with it. "I'll take it!" she told the assistant.

He told her the price, convinced it would be too much for the poor woman.

Witch Nightshade took out a large, flat purse that looked completely empty, and to the shop assistant's astonishment began pulling five-pound notes from it. He took the notes and held them up to the light before putting them in his till, not trusting them to be genuine.

Satisfied, the shop assistant gave her a receipt. Then he picked up a large cardboard box from behind the counter.

"No need to pack it," said Witch Nightshade. "I'll ride it home."

"Ride it?" exclaimed the bemused shop assistant, who was beginning to feel a bit dazed and wasn't at all sure whether or not he was having a bad dream.

"It shouldn't be too difficult to handle, though I know it's not quite what I'm used to," said the witch, and settling herself on the handle of the cleaner, she immediately zoomed out of the shop – slowly at first, and weaving just a little – leaving the shocked young man staring after her.

Seconds later, Witch Nightshade had vanished from sight.

Wiping his hand across his eyes, the shop assistant decided it was time for a soothing cup of tea. He couldn't believe what he had just seen.

But the poor man was even more amazed later on, when a crowd of very oddly-dressed ladies came into his shop, demanding every last one of his vacuum cleaners.

Witch Nightshade had certainly caused a sensation at her coven: all the witches wanted their own new-fangled broomsticks!

THE LAST WIZARD

Believe it or not, the last magical wizard in the land was a little boy whose name was Mervyn. Like all wizards, he was the seventh son of a seventh son.

For a time, Mervyn enjoyed it. He became very popular at school, because he could work a spell to make everyone's maths homework correct. And he could make sure that his school football team always won their matches.

But gradually Mervyn grew rather tired of working spells for all his friends. In fact, he rather wished he wasn't a wizard. He didn't like to be different from all the other children, and he hated it when they kept pestering him to work spells.

"I don't want to be a wizard any more," Mervyn told his parents one day. They were having dinner at the time. "I'm fed up with being different and always being asked to cast spells to prove I'm a wizard," he grumbled. He just wanted to be like his friends.

"Once a wizard, always a wizard," said his mum, putting down her fork and wagging a finger at him. "You ought to be pleased to be the only real wizard left in the land."

Mervyn scowled and pushed his sausages round his plate. He couldn't even be bothered to make them stand up and do a jig for him. He wasn't at all pleased to be the last wizard!

13

In fact, Mervyn was so fed up that he confided in his best friend, Darren.

"I don't know what to do, Darren," he said. "I've got this great big spell book that belonged to my great-great-grandfather, and it makes me cast spells from it, even if I don't want to."

Darren thought about it, then had a brilliant idea. "How about if I borrow the book from you," he said, "and then sort of lose it?"

"Mum and Dad would be furious," said Mervyn. "And what do you mean, lose it? It mustn't get into the wrong hands."

"Trust me," said Darren.

So the next day Mervyn lent Darren the book and it conveniently disappeared. Without it, Mervyn felt quite relieved as he was now unable to work any spells at all.

His parents were furious, of course, but nothing could be done. So what had happened to the spell book?

Thousands of miles away in Australia, Darren's aunt was celebrating her birthday. Eagerly she unwrapped the heavy parcel from her nephew.

"A spell book!" she exclaimed in delight. "Just what I've always wanted!" She couldn't wait to begin. For Darren's aunt was the seventh daughter of a seventh daughter!

THE LOST RABBIT

On the day of Simon's birthday party his pet rabbit, Thumper –
a beautiful white angora – disappeared. Simon found the hutch
door open and realised he couldn't have latched it properly.

He was sure Thumper had been stolen.

How could Simon enjoy his party, now? He was far too
worried about his rabbit. When his friends arrived,
all he could manage was the most
watery of smiles. To make matters worse,
his friend Carla gave him a special brush for
Thumper. Simon thanked her in a
very small, wobbly voice.

He cheered up a little when they went
in to tea and he blew out the seven red
candles on his birthday cake shaped
like a train.

He brightened up even more
when his mum led them all into
the living-room for Simon's surprise
present.

When he and his friends had
taken their places round the
floor, a very strange-looking
character swept imperiously
into the room. He wore a
long blue robe decorated
with silver stars, and a
tall black hat.

It was a conjuror!

"Magician," he said, correcting one of Simon's friends, who asked him if he was the same conjuror his mum had booked for his own party the following week.

"I only visit an area once," said the magician, mysteriously. "Too much strong magic in the atmosphere is very bad."

A wonderful display of magic followed. The magician waved his wand and the children all gasped as flowered wallpaper became a living garden with the flowers blowing gently in the breeze. Then a troupe of ballet dancers suddenly waltzed right out of the television set! Soon the ballet dancers disappeared, giving way to an amazing firework display.

Finally, the magician produced a shiny, black top hat.

"You're the birthday boy," he said, turning to Simon. "What would you like me to bring out of my magic hat? Don't tell anyone what it is."

Simon shut his eyes and wished and wished.

The magician waved his wand, and out of his hat came…

"Thumper!" shouted Simon, jumping up.

Simon recognised him at once, for he was pure white and had a black spot under his chin. He took Thumper from the magician and cuddled the rabbit in his arms.

Could the magician have stolen him? Simon didn't think so. He had used real magic, not just conjuring tricks. No, somehow the magician's magic had brought Thumper right back home from wherever he had been.

Simon may never know what had happened to Thumper but he knew he couldn't have wished for a better birthday present, and when he went to bed that night his head was full of strange and mysterious dreams!

FELICITY WITCH

Felicity Witch lived in an old cottage at the edge of a dark wood, with her cat, Midnight. She was a well-meaning witch and got on well with the local villagers, who were rather proud to have a witch living among them.

One day, she received a letter from Chief Witch Hemlock.

You are summonsed to appear before the coven next Friday, 13th May, at midnight prompt.
DO NOT BE LATE!

Felicity trembled with alarm. A summons from the Chief Witch usually meant trouble. But as far as Felicity knew, she was a good witch and hadn't done anything wrong.

She did have rather more visitors than was usual for a witch, it's true: every Tuesday afternoon she held a tea party for the ladies in the village. They not only loved her blackberry tea – they all actually liked Felicity Witch, despite her scruffy clothes and unfortunate appearance.

Felicity arrived early at the coven and greeted her sister witches with her usual sweet smile as they flew down on their broomsticks. They smiled back cheerfully, which made Felicity Witch feel better. Perhaps she wasn't in trouble after all.

Then Chief Witch Hemlock arrived. She was a tall, skinny, rather bad-tempered witch with piercing black eyes and a hairy chin.

Seeing all the witches talking and catching up on the news together in a friendly fashion, she stormed furiously into the middle of the gathering.

"This is all your doing, Felicity Witch!" she screeched.

"What is?" asked Felicity.

"All this laughing and being nice. It's just not witch-like. It makes friends of enemies," said the Chief Witch sourly.

"But I don't have any enemies," said Felicity Witch, smiling sweetly.

"There you go again! Stop it!" snapped Chief Witch Hemlock.

"I can't," said Felicity. "It's part of me. Perhaps it's because my mother called me Felicity. It means 'happiness'."

"Then we'll just have to change your name," said Chief Witch Hemlock. "We'll call you… Wartsnap!"

Felicity stopped smiling. "That's an ugly name!"

"Too bad!" said Chief Witch Hemlock. "At least it's stopped you smiling! I'm Chief Witch, so what I say, goes!"

20

Poor Felicity flew home again in tears. She was so miserable with her horrible new name that it changed her completely and she found it hard to smile.

On Tuesday afternoon, when the ladies came round, they found her hunched, haggard and unhappy. But because they knew Felicity so well, they put their arms round her and hugged her.

"Cheer up," they said. "Give us one of your lovely smiles."

Felicity managed a very weak one.

"That's better. Now put your feet up, and we'll make you a cup of tea."

The kindness and concern of her friends made Felicity suddenly realise something.

"It's who you are that matters," she thought. "Not your name!"

And she gave her Tuesday afternoon ladies one of her most dazzling and beautiful smiles ever.

THE DAISY RING

Mr Trimble loved neatness, especially in his garden. He had wonderful displays of flowers and not a weed or bug in sight. But his pride and joy was his lawn: it was immaculate.

One morning, Mr Trimble looked out of his bedroom window and gasped. There was a ring of daisies in the middle of his beautiful lawn!

Straight away, he fetched his lawnmower and ran it over the daisies. Then he sprinkled weedkiller on them.

"That'll fix 'em!"

But the very next morning the daisy ring was back.

Over the next few weeks, Mr Trimble tried every way to get rid of that daisy ring, but without success. Each morning it returned, and seemed to him to be looking bigger and stronger.

Now foolish Mr Trimble thought he would rather have no lawn at all than one spoiled by daisies. So he laid paving stones over the lot and called it his patio.

"I can always put pots of plants on it," he said to himself.

That night, he was woken up by the sound of hammers on stone. He went to the window and saw an astonishing sight.

A group of tiny people were in the middle of his patio, attacking it with pickaxes.

Furious, Mr Trimble threw on his dressing-gown and stormed into the garden.

"What do you think you're doing?" he yelled. "You're ruining my new patio."

A tiny little fellow, no bigger than Mr Trimble's foot, stood with his arms folded, looking very cross indeed.

"Never mind your patio – you worry about your garden!" he said. "Our daisy ring can't push through all these stones!"

"Good job, too!" growled Mr Trimble.

"So that's all the thanks we get!" the little man screeched, dancing with rage. "Who do you think makes your grass so green, your plants grow so well and keeps away all the slugs and caterpillars?"

"Er… I suppose…"

"It's us, you silly great oaf! We do it. But if there's no fairy ring, we can't come."

Mr Trimble had no idea these little people were responsible for his garden! Now he had to decide whether to have no daisies or no garden! If he destroyed the fairy ring, he could say goodbye to all his prize flowers and vegetables.

"All right," he said, reluctantly. "I'll get rid of the paving stones."

In time Mr Trimble even grew to love the daisy ring. It was really quite a pretty feature in the middle of his immaculate lawn.

PLAYING WIZARDS

Harry's uncle was a wizard. He could cast spells and even turn bottle tops into coins. This made Harry very popular at school, because everyone thought that Harry must be a wizard, too.

"Come on, Harry," pleaded Sam. "Just do one little spell."

"I'm not a wizard," Harry insisted. "I can't do any magic."

"I bet you could if you tried," said Sam. "Ask your uncle to show you, or borrow his spell book!"

Sam went on so much that in the end, the next time Harry visited his uncle, he asked him if he could turn Buttercup the canary into a vulture, and then back again. He didn't like the idea of borrowing the spell book to try it himself.

Harry watched his uncle very carefully, taking note of all the ingredients he used and the magic words he muttered as he dabbed the mixture over the canary's feathers.

In minutes, Buttercup had changed into a large vulture with a rather surprised expression.

Harry paid very careful attention to his uncle as he reversed the spell on the vulture. He was rather scared that he might get it wrong when he tried it himself.

25

Next day, Harry and Sam met in Harry's den at the bottom of the garden. Sam had brought his hamster with him because neither of them had a canary.

Harry looked at the piece of paper on which he had scribbled down the ingredients for the spell. Some of them were too difficult to find – Amazonian creeper leaves, for instance – so he made do with something similar instead.

"I expect they'll work," said Harry, confidently adding leaves from the creeper on the side of the house.

Harry stirred the disgusting mixture, muttering the words he'd heard his uncle use. Then he dabbed it on the hamster.

The hamster began to grow larger and larger.

"It's working!" said Harry.

"I can't see any sign of a beak," said Sam, backing nervously away from his giant pet.

The hamster's little nose was stretching into a trunk, and his ears were getting wide and flat.

"Help," gasped Harry. "It's not changing into a vulture at all! It's much too big. I think it's going to be an elephant!"

Soon the shed was too small for them all, so the boys opened the door and backed out.

That was a mistake.

Before Harry had time to reverse the spell, the hamster-elephant gave an enormous trumpeting cry and charged out of the shed and through the garden gate. On the way, it smashed the bowl containing the spell mixture and flattened Dad's cabbages.

"Stop him!" yelled Harry, as the two boys rushed after the trumpeting elephant.

But by the time the two boys reached the gate, the elephant was out of sight.

Luckily, Harry's uncle always put a safety element into his spells in case they got into the wrong hands. So he wasn't too surprised when the elephant arrived at his front door. In no time at all Sam's hamster was restored to its former self. Harry's uncle telephoned Harry and asked him to collect it.

"Never mess around with spells," he told Harry firmly. "If you can't get a spell absolutely right, just don't try it at all." And Harry very sensibly promised that he wouldn't.

THE WITCH TRAP

There was once a very unpleasant witch called Dreadnought, who spent all her time adding more and more horrid spells to her great leather-bound spell book.

She had spells to change dogs into centipedes, or a delicious beef stew into a mouldy mess. She could even transform a young bride on her wedding day into a bent old hag.

"We have to do something to stop her from making our lives a misery," said Mayor Nettletwist, who had just had his state coach turned into a rusty wheelbarrow.

All the citizens of the town agreed. They had all suffered from the witch's nasty spells. But what could they do?

The Mayor had a plan. "We'll burn the old witch's spell book," he said, "and at the same time, we'll give her a fright she'll never forget."

As it happened, every Monday morning, Witch Dreadnought walked across the fields to Chestnut Wood to collect ingredients for her spells: dead flies, toadstools and anything else that took her fancy. She always took the same route.

One particular Monday, she was making her way to the wood as usual, when there was a loud *crack*! and a *crash*! – and the witch fell into a big hole that had been hidden under branches and leaves.

She had, of course, left her spell book at home, so she could not magic herself out of the hole.

All the townsfolk hurried across the field to see the horrid old witch ranting and raving in her prison. The Mayor stood at the edge of the hole and laughed, while the old witch screeched fit to burst.

"Let me out, or I'll make warts grow all over your noses! I'll–"

"Oh, no you won't," said the Mayor. "You can't because we've taken your spell book!"

Mr Chop, the butcher, held the book over the hole for her to see.

The witch was furious, but there was nothing she could do. There was no danger that the villagers would use the book – they didn't know how to work spells. But she still couldn't get out of the hole.

She sat crouched in the darkness, wondering what was going on. They were doing something… she could smell smoke!

Oh no! They were lighting a fire!

"Are you ready for your punishment, Witch Dreadnought?" asked the Mayor.

Witch Dreadnought was terrified. She began to shiver and shake. What were they going to do? She shivered and shook so much, her hat fell off.

"It's burning! It's burning!" cried someone, and then Witch Dreadnought realised that her precious spell book was being burned on the fire!

But the Mayor was not really an unkind man: he suddenly felt sorry for the witch. Without her magic she was just a little old woman. "Will you promise never to have another spell book?" he asked Witch Dreadnought.

"No!" she cried. "A witch must have a spell book!"

"Very well, then. But only one with helpful spells," said the Mayor.

"What fun are they?" thought the witch. Then she smelled the burnt leather of her book and thought of what might happen to her if she didn't agree. They might leave her in this hole for ever! "Very well," she said. "I promise."

So the Mayor threw a rope down to her and helped her climb out.

Witch Dreadnought bought a new spell book. It contained recipes for potions and creams, and spells for curing and healing and making the ugly beautiful.

She made friends and began to enjoy helping people, and after a while she became known as the Good Witch Cure-all.

THE TRAVELLING WITCH

Wanda Witch flung her cloak round her, rammed her hat on to her head and, calling her cat, she went out into her back yard to collect her broomstick. She sat astride it with Blackberry, her cat, perched behind, and commanded her broom to take them to Humpty Bumpty Hill. But the broomstick didn't so much as twitch a twig.

Wanda kicked it angrily. "Get going!" she screeched, shaking the handle. "We'll be late for the coven!"

But the broomstick did not budge.

"The magic must have worn out," said Wanda at last. "Well, there's no time to work a revival spell now. What am I going to do, Blackberry? I can't miss the meeting – they're going to choose a new Chief Witch!"

"You could go by rail," said Blackberry.

By rail? Now there was a thought. It would ruin her image, of course, but Wanda didn't have much choice. Her broom was well and truly unmagicked.

She put Blackberry into his travel basket and ran down to the railway station.

33

She rushed into the station and put Blackberry's basket down on the floor.

"A return ticket to Humpty Bumpty Hill!" she snapped at the ticket man. "When's the next train?"

"Never heard of it. Ask the ticket collector." He looked doubtfully at Wanda. "Are you off to some fancy dress party?"

"Of course not!" said Wanda irritably, grabbing her ticket. She could hear a train approaching. "You must have heard of Humpty Bumpty Hill. It's famous," she said to the ticket collector. "Tell me quickly, or I'll turn you into a toad!"

Fortunately, there was a lady behind her who did know the place and she gave Wanda directions. Barely thanking her, Wanda sped on to the platform.

"Don't forget me!" wailed Blackberry from his basket. But Wanda didn't hear him. She flung open the door of a carriage and leaped on, just as the train was beginning to move.

At the same time, a sudden gust of wind sent her pointed hat bowling away along the platform.

Wanda Witch left the train at Chatterbox Junction, as the lady had directed her, and soon saw the familiar shape of Humpty Bumpty Hill ahead.

The coven was just beginning. Fifty witches were gathered there, each with her own black cat.

Wanda Witch arrived, hatless, catless and without her broomstick.

The Chief Witch frowned.

"What have we here?" she asked. "An outsider? Away with you – this coven is for witches only!"

"But I'm Wanda Witch!" said Wanda. "You all know me!"

"Wanda Witch? Nonsense!" said the Chief Witch. "Wanda Witch has a broomstick, a black cat and a tall hat. You have none of these things."

Wanda tried to tell them all about her broomstick, the train, and about poor Blackberry whom she had left behind in the station. But they wouldn't listen. They all got to their feet and shooed her away with their broomsticks.

Wanda Witch fled.

She had a long wait at the station for the next train. And when she got back to her own station she found Blackberry sitting comfortably on a station bench.

"I'm staying here," he said. "I'm fed up with being a witch's cat. I want to be a station cat instead."

So Wanda Witch returned to her cottage without her cat and without her hat. The Chief Witch had said she couldn't be a witch without these things. Well, perhaps she wouldn't be a witch any more. Perhaps she would join the Senior Citizens' Club and go on outings to Blackpool…

Wanda Witch felt a whole new life was just beginning…

THE SPELLING BOOK

Jenny found the book on a second-hand bookstall. It had a worn, red leather cover and SPELLING BOOK printed in black letters. She hoped it would contain lists of difficult words she could learn to spell. But when she got home and opened it, the book had nothing but funny-looking squiggles and numbers in it. No words at all!

Jenny was very disappointed.

"What's the use of a spelling book if I can't read it?" she said, throwing the book to the back of her bedroom cupboard.

But that wasn't the end of it.

The next week she went back to the bookstall to look for something better.

"I hope you've got something I can read this time," she joked to the sales assistant. "That spelling book was useless!"

"Did you say spelling book?" asked the assistant. "Was it covered in red leather with big black lettering?"

"That's it," said Jenny.

"Thank goodness! It's Mr Merlin's book – it was brought here by mistake and he needs it back!"

"He can have it," said Jenny. "It's no good to me."

"Would you be a dear and return it to him? You can choose a couple of free books instead to make up for it."

Jenny chose her two books and the assistant gave her Mr Merlin's address.

After lunch, Jenny and her mother took the book round to his house. The door had a funny brass knocker on it shaped like a dragon. Jenny was sure it winked at her when she knocked, and she felt just a little bit afraid.

Mr Merlin opened the door. He was tall and thin, with a long white beard and big bushy eyebrows over piercing blue eyes.

"Hello, Mr Merlin," said Jenny. "We've brought your spelling book back."

The old man's face lit up. "You've found it! Thank goodness! I can't do my job without it."

Jenny suddenly realised what the book really was. "It's for magic spells, isn't it?" she said.

"It is indeed," said Mr Merlin, gravely taking the book from her. "It contains all the magic spells I could possibly need. Enough magic to create anything you can dream of. I'm a wizard, you see. But come inside, both of you. I must give you a reward for returning it to me."

Jenny and her mum followed Mr Merlin into the house. An owl was asleep on a perch in the corner.

"Now, what would you like best in all the world?" asked Mr Merlin. "I can make anything happen for you."

It was tempting to ask for a pony, or lots of money and a palace to live in, but Jenny remembered from fairy tales that wishes like these things seldom worked out satisfactorily. She thought of something that would be far more useful to her.

"I'd like to be able to spell," she said. "Words, that is, not making magic spells."

Mr Merlin nodded his head. "Oh, that's easy," he said. He opened his book, found a page and muttered a few strange words. A wisp of purple smoke whirled round Jenny's head.

"There! Now you'll be the best speller in the land!" he told her. "And because you didn't ask me for anything very extravagant, I have given you one magic wish as well. Use it wisely!"

And Jenny, being a very sensible little girl, did just that.

39

FAIRY CAKES

Jiminy Goblin was passing the baker's one day when he saw some little cakes in the window. He went inside and asked the baker what they were.

"Fairy cakes," the baker replied.

They looked delicious: golden, with tiny strands of sugar sprinkled over them. Two thin slices of cake stood upright in a little paper case, like little fairy wings, set with a generous scoop of fresh cream. Jiminy couldn't resist buying some.

"I'll take a dozen," he said.

But as he was preparing his tea, his mouth watering at the thought of the little cakes waiting to be eaten, something occurred to him.

"Fairy cakes. Does that mean they are enchanted? Will I change into something horrible if I eat them? Perhaps I'll change into a fairy." Jiminy shuddered at the thought. But it gave him an idea.

He decided not to eat the fairy cakes after all, but to make some of his own. "I'll call them goblin cakes. And I'll put my own special spell in them that will turn whoever eats them into my servants! Ha ha!"

Jiminy made the goblin cakes and invited
three of his least favourite goblin friends round to tea.

"Do have a cake," he told them.

"Yum-yum. These are delicious, Jiminy," said Lennie Loafer,
greedily reaching for another.

The plate of cakes disappeared fast, and within minutes,
Jiminy had three helpers running round his cottage, doing all
the jobs he hated doing himself. They grumbled all the time,
but because of the spell, they could not stop working, and there
was plenty to do because Jiminy was a very untidy goblin.

Jiminy Goblin took a deckchair into the garden and stretched
out in the sun.

A short time later a young man who looked like a traveller –
but who happened to be a wizard – stopped by his gate.

"Hello there! Could you spare a
traveller a cup of tea?"

"Certainly," said Jiminy Goblin,
and he went to the kitchen door.
"Gentleman here wants a cuppa!"
he shouted to his helpers. "Give
him one of my cakes as well." For
Jiminy figured that having four
helpers would be even better
than having three.

"A cake!" said the young man in surprise. "I've never been offered cake before. Usually I'm lucky to get a glass of water." He picked up the cake and studied it. "Hmm," he said, thoughtfully. He looked through the cottage window and smiled. "I think you're trying to put me under some kind of spell, like those poor people in there."

"Me?" said Jiminy Goblin, feigning surprise. "A spell?"

"Well, if you're not, then prove it. Take a bite of the cake yourself," said the young man. "A big bite."

"Glad to," said Jiminy, for his spell would only affect other people. He took a mouthful of cake. The young man suddenly made a strange movement with his hand. He then turned towards the gate and beckoned to Jiminy. Jiminy Goblin found himself following, even though he didn't want to.

"You are a very foolish goblin," said the young man, as he walked down the lane with Jiminy walking behind. "You are now my servant, for I have turned your spell back on itself. A wizard needs a good servant, wouldn't you agree?"

Jiminy Goblin had to follow the wizard out of town, walking close behind him and doing everything he was told to do. His three friends worked hard in the cottage until their spells wore off. And so far as anyone knows, Jiminy is the wizard's servant to this very day.

42

THE HALLOWE'EN PARTY

"Now, children," said Miss Partridge, "next Tuesday is Hallowe'en, and we're going to have a big party with plenty of games!"

"Great!" said Jack, who had been to one before and scared everyone with his monster mask.

"Everyone should dress up," Miss Partridge went on, "and I'd like you each to bring some fun things for us to eat. Sausages made to look like broomsticks, for instance, and oranges carved with funny faces."

All the children were excited, except Lizzie Wimple. She told Miss Partridge she was too busy that evening to come.

"Too busy for a Hallowe'en party?" queried Jack as they got ready to leave.

"Hallowe'en is always a busy time at home," she explained.

As soon as she got home, Lizzie told her mum about the party. "But it will be pathetic," she said. "I know it will. All of them dressing up in silly costumes, and not a bit of real magic anywhere."

Lizzie's mother smiled. "Well, we could do something about that," she said.

"But I said I wasn't going," said Lizzie.

"Think about it. You could do something special to surprise them all." Lizzie's mum was one of those witches that believed in using magic to entertain, not to do nasty tricks on people.

43

"All right," said Lizzie. "But could you bake me a special cake?"

The next day at school Lizzie told Miss Partridge that she would be coming to the party after all.

Hallowe'en came. By six o'clock, all the children had arrived – dressed as ghosts, witches, skeletons, vampires and other amazing monsters. There was delicious food, too: someone had even brought a cake with black icing and blue stars on it!

"Time to light the lanterns," said Miss Partridge. They all went out into the playground, where pumpkin lanterns were arranged along the walls. With their flickering candles, they made the playground look magical and mysterious.

But then, just as the children were about to go inside for the first games, they heard a whirring, swishing noise in the air. They looked up… and saw Lizzie Wimple dressed as a witch, flying across the playing fields towards them.

"Wow!" said Jack. "She's flying on a broomstick! I wonder how she makes it work."

"It must be magic!" said Kate, who believed in such things.

Lizzie flew round the playground once, did a loop-the-loop, then landed expertly. Everyone crowded round, admiring the broom and wishing they could have a go.

Lizzie offered a ride to the smallest child in the school.

"It's only a small broomstick," she explained. "It wouldn't be able to carry anyone bigger, as well as me."

But the most magical part of the evening came when the mysterious black cake was cut. Jack was the first to try it. If he hadn't believed in magic before, he certainly did now. The cake tasted of all the best things he had ever eaten.

When he'd finished it, he felt he wanted to rush into the playground and take to the air.

And that's just what he did – without even a broomstick or a pair of wings!

Soon everyone had eaten some of the amazing cake and the air was filled with flying children and teachers!

They all agreed that it was a truly wonderful Hallowe'en party.

"Well," said Lizzie to herself, getting back on to her broomstick, "I always knew Mum baked light cakes, but she must have used masses of self-raising flour for this one!"

THE NEW BROOM

Hattie Hickory lived in a crooked old cottage with dark rooms and cobwebs in every corner. Dusty old books of spells spilled from shelves and covered every inch of spare floor space. Cupboards were stuffed with pills and potion bottles. Bunches of dried herbs hung from every beam. It was all very untidy, but that's how Hattie liked it.

But one day Hattie Hickory tripped over a pile of books and spilled a whole bottle of wart cure over her best broomstick. Immediately, the bristles shrivelled and fell off the stick.

"Botherations!" she cried. "Now I need a new broom."

"What you need," said her cat, Spitfire, "is an assistant."

An assistant! What a good idea!

"I'll advertise for one," said Hattie Hickory.

A week later, Daphne Doogood arrived. She was a neat, plump lady with a brisk, no-nonsense manner. She wasn't quite the sort of person Hattie had in mind. She would have preferred someone she could boss about, but Daphne would have to do, as nobody else had applied for the position.

"I'm off into town to buy a new broomstick," Hattie told Daphne on her first morning. "I want you to tidy the spell books and then arrange all the potions in alphabetical order, so that I can find them easily."

Daphne Doogood was delighted. She loved tidying up and organising things.

Hattie Hickory's shopping trip took rather longer than she expected. She was very particular when it came to broomsticks, and determined to find exactly the right one for her. Then she'd had to get a spell to enable the broom to fly.

When at last she arrived back home, she wondered if she'd come to the right place.

The cottage windows were flung wide open. Freshly-washed curtains were drying on the line. The hedge had been neatly trimmed and the herb garden weeded. When Hattie pushed the cottage door open she smelled disinfectant and furniture polish.

Her living room was unrecognisable. It was clean and bright, with not a cobweb or speck of dust in sight. The furniture gleamed and a vase of yellow daffodils stood on the table.

Not even Spitfire had escaped. She cowered under the table, her fur washed and brushed and a velvet collar round her neck.

Daphne Doogood was just tipping Hattie's collection of stuffed toads into the dustbin.

"What have you done?" gasped Hattie Hickory.

Daphne Doogood beamed at her. "Doesn't it look so much better? You could eat a meal off your floor now. Oh, and I've cleared out all those dusty old books on to a bonfire."

"Oh, no!" Hattie Hickory felt faint. She dashed out of the kitchen door and into the back garden. It was true! A bonfire was burning merrily, and she could see the remains of her spell books crackling and sparking as they turned black and crumbled into ashes.

Turning to Daphne, who was busily trimming the grass and taking no notice, Hattie Hickory spluttered furiously.

"I'll turn you into a rat! I'll make your teeth fall out! I'll give you purple boils…"

But, of course, she could do none of these things: she had no spell books.

Spitfire grinned down at Hattie from the top of the garden wall. She was feeling much better. "Miaow! They do say there's nothing like a new broom to sweep away old and unwanted things," she said with a smirk. "Well, it seems you have two new brooms now!"

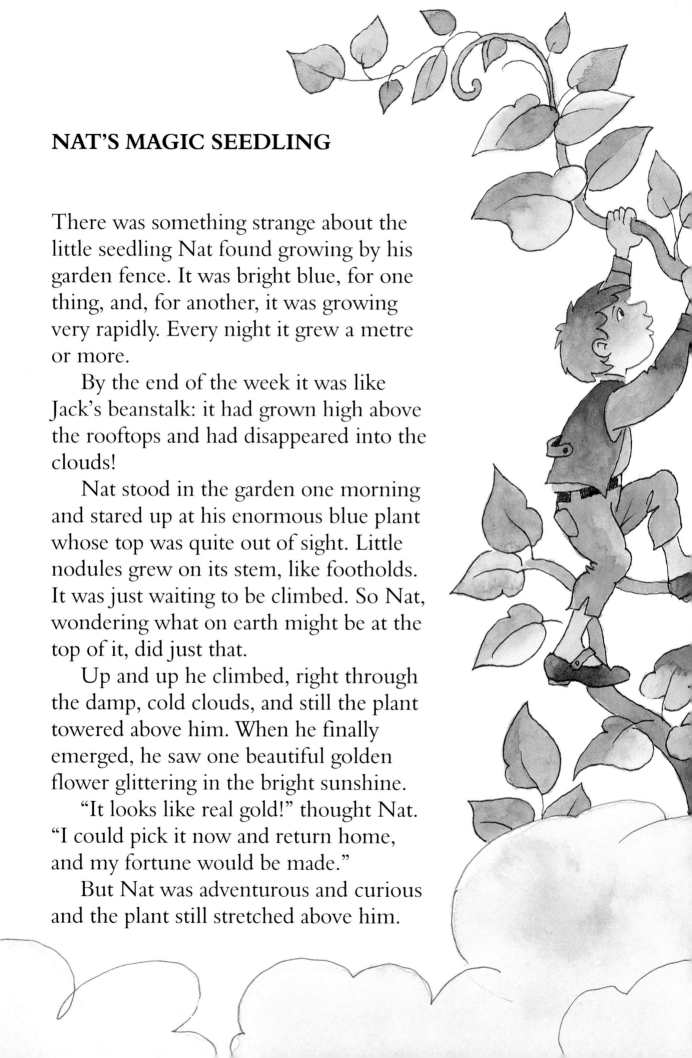

NAT'S MAGIC SEEDLING

There was something strange about the little seedling Nat found growing by his garden fence. It was bright blue, for one thing, and, for another, it was growing very rapidly. Every night it grew a metre or more.

By the end of the week it was like Jack's beanstalk: it had grown high above the rooftops and had disappeared into the clouds!

Nat stood in the garden one morning and stared up at his enormous blue plant whose top was quite out of sight. Little nodules grew on its stem, like footholds. It was just waiting to be climbed. So Nat, wondering what on earth might be at the top of it, did just that.

Up and up he climbed, right through the damp, cold clouds, and still the plant towered above him. When he finally emerged, he saw one beautiful golden flower glittering in the bright sunshine.

"It looks like real gold!" thought Nat. "I could pick it now and return home, and my fortune would be made."

But Nat was adventurous and curious and the plant still stretched above him.

So Nat left the golden flower where it was and climbed on until he finally came to the blue, feathery top of the plant.

He was not really surprised when he found that he could step off the plant and stand on the cloud around it. He expected to see a castle, too. But something quite different came out of the mist.

It was clearly a wizard. He wore a splendid cloak of deep midnight blue with golden stars, and a tall, black, conical hat.

They stared at each other.

"Have you anything in your pocket?" demanded the wizard.

"N… not much," Nat replied nervously, remembering how he had nearly been tempted into picking the golden flower. He pulled out a dirty handkerchief, a corkscrew and a penny whistle.

"No golden flower?" asked the wizard.

Nat shook his head.

To his surprise, the wizard laughed delightedly.

51

"Splendid!" he said. "That's why you are the only person ever to have reached the top of the plant. Everyone else who climbed the plant has always stopped to pick the golden flower and take it home. Much good it did them, for as soon as they put their feet on the ground, it turned to dust. Now at last I've met someone whose natural curiosity is greater than their greed."

The wizard took a small wooden box from his pocket and handed it to Nat.

"Inside this box is another seed. Plant it and look after it carefully, and it will soon grow to the height of a sunflower, and bloom twice a year. Don't give it any water. Clean the leaves regularly with metal polish, and sing it a lullaby each night."

Nat thanked the wizard and waved goodbye. He quickly climbed back down the plant and did exactly what the wizard instructed. Before long, a small blue shoot appeared. And by the end of the summer, Nat had picked bunch after bunch of pure golden flowers.

THE BROOMSTICK RACE

Mr Troopuddle specialised in making broomsticks for witches. But it didn't make him much money because he didn't sell very many. Witches were becoming rather scarce, and those that were around seldom bought new brooms. Things were getting rather desperate for poor Mr Troopuddle. He wondered how he could continue making a living out of selling witches' brooms.

Then one day he had a bright idea: he would run a broomstick race, and the prize would be a special, luxury broom.

It took him many days to complete, but the prize broom was his very finest creation: it had a polished wooden handle, carved at the top into a cat's head, and beautifully-laid, oiled willow twigs. It stood in the window of his shop, together with a poster giving details of the race.

Before long, every single witch in the land had heard about the race – and the wonderful broomstick that would go to the winner. Soon they were queuing to sign up for the race.

The day of the race was dull and windy. The competitors set off eagerly on their decrepit old broomsticks, but unfortunately some never made it beyond Nightshade Woods before their broomsticks fell apart. Some lost their way among the heavy clouds. Some simply fell off. Only three made it to the finishing line outside Mr Troopuddle's shop, and the winner was Witch Hellebore.

She snatched the prize broomstick with greedy glee, knowing she would be the envy of every witch in the land.

"Aren't there any consolation prizes?" grumbled the two runners up.

Mr Troopuddle quickly gave them brand-new brooms from his standard range.

"I want one like Hellebore's!" wailed Witch Muckleberry.

"So do I!" shouted Witch Batswing.

"I'd be delighted to make another two for you," said Mr Troopuddle, carefully.

The two witches considered. They'd have to pay for them, of course, but it was worth it to have new brooms just like Hellebore's.

Mr Troopuddle's plan worked better than he dreamed possible. None of the witches wanted to be outdone by her sisters. Before long, every single witch who had attended the race had ordered a new deluxe broomstick. His fortune made, Mr Troopuddle retired to a comfortable little cottage in the country, and never had to work again.

THE MAGIC BICYCLE

The bicycle Ellie received on her eighth birthday looked perfectly ordinary. It was black with a large, shiny silver bell. At first she had been very disappointed because she had so wanted a pony. But when Ellie looked more closely, she found a little cluster of golden stars just under the saddle. They made it rather special.

Ellie asked her mum where she had bought it.

"That funny little shop at the end of the High Street," her mum replied.

Ellie knew the shop. It was full of old and dusty second-hand bicycles that made hers look smart by comparison.

"It was a bargain!" said Mum. "It looks almost new, but it was ridiculously cheap."

"Hmmm," thought Ellie. "Strange." But she couldn't wait to try it out. She decided to ride down the hill to the village on it.

She checked out the brakes before she set out, put on her safety gear and set off for Steeplechase Hill.

The hill was very steep and scary, with a sharp bend at the bottom. As Ellie went whizzing down it at top speed, she squeezed on the brake handles – but nothing happened! Faster and faster went the bike, with Ellie hanging on grimly.

When they reached the bottom, something extraordinary happened: the bicycle gave a little buck – and leaped right across the bend to where the road straightened out again!

"Wow!" thought Ellie. "That was neat."

She patted her bike absent-mindedly as though it were a pony. It certainly acted like one. As she rode down towards the village it kept giving excited little bucks and tossing its handlebars. Ellie even thought she could hear it whinnying.

Back home, she looked again at the little stars under the saddle and saw they were horseshoe-shaped. She hadn't noticed that before. "I bet I'm the only person in the world with a pony-bicycle," thought Ellie.

Every day Ellie took her bicycle for a canter. Sometimes they went across the fields and vaulted the hedges. Sometimes they climbed the downs. She was sure that if she treated her bicycle just as if it were a pony for long enough, then one day it might turn into one.

Curiously, Ellie was seen to be riding a neat little bay pony in the village last week – so perhaps it did.

THE MONSTER UNDER THE PAVEMENT

Kerry saw monsters everywhere: in the airing cupboard, under the bed, and even behind her wardrobe.

"There are no such things as monsters," her mum said, the day Kerry ran in to tell her that the airing cupboard monster was curled up on top of the spare duvet. "It's probably the cat."

But Kerry knew better.

Then one morning, as Kerry and her mum were walking to the shops, a pair of skinny hands poked up from a manhole in the pavement and grabbed Kerry's ankles.

"Mum!" screamed Kerry. "A monster's grabbed me!"

"Don't be silly, dear," said Kerry's mum. She was walking ahead, studying her shopping list and didn't notice Kerry being dragged out of sight behind her.

Kerry dropped into the hole and landed uncomfortably in a cold, underground stream with a loud splash. Then something pulled her from the water and put her on a narrow ledge.

Kerry opened her eyes. She saw a small monster with three eyes, fluffy black fur and huge pink ears.

"What do you want?" asked Kerry, nervously.

"We want our friends back," said the monster.

"Well, what can I do about it?"

"They're trapped in your airing cupboard, under your bed, and behind your wardrobe," replied the monster. "Didn't you notice them?"

Kerry admitted she had been too scared to look properly.

"You just need to set them free," said the monster. "Then lift up the manhole cover so they can come home."

It didn't sound too difficult.

The monster took Kerry's hand and helped her back up the long ladder to the surface again.

"Goodbye," he said. "Don't forget, now."

As if she could!

Mum was still standing on the pavement, trying to work out if she'd written "potatoes" or "tomatoes", as Kerry climbed back out of the manhole.

"Hi, Mum!"

"Oh, there you are, dear," said Mum. "I thought you'd gone home again."

"Um… if you don't mind, I think I will," said Kerry. "I have something important to do."

"All right, dear," said her mother. "But don't get in Gran's way."

"I won't!" promised Kerry. She ran back home and rang the doorbell.

"I'm just baking a cake," said Gran cheerfully, when she opened the door to her.

"I won't get in the way!" said Kerry as she ran straight upstairs, happy that the coast was clear for her to look for the sewer monster's friends.

She went first to the airing cupboard. The monster inside was tangled up in a shirt. Kerry carefully untangled the shirtsleeve round its neck and the monster hopped out.

"Come with me," said Kerry, "and be very quiet."

In her bedroom, the under-the-bed monster was stuck to the floor by a lump of chewing gum. Kerry carefully unstuck him.

The monster behind the wardrobe had its fur caught on a nail. Kerry snipped it free with her scissors.

"Come on, quickly!" she said to the three monsters, and they followed her down the stairs, out of the door, and along the pavement to the manhole.

Kerry had to struggle a bit to lift the cover, but the monsters wasted no time in jumping down into the black hole. She heard three splashes as they landed at the bottom.

Three sets of eyes looked up at her in the gloom, and very faintly she heard a big cheer.

THE MAGIC STONE

It was Jason who found the stone lying in the gutter.

"It's just a stone," said Evie, looking at the plain, grey pebble in her brother's hand.

"But it's completely round, like a ball," said Jason.

"Throw it away," Evie told him. "You've enough junk as it is."

But Jason put it in his pocket and forgot about it.

That night, whilst he was lying in bed, reading his favourite book, Jason became aware of a  strange light filling his bedroom. It seemed to be coming from his jeans tossed over the chair. Then he remembered the stone.

He got out of bed, thrust his hand into his jeans pocket and pulled the stone free.

It shone so brilliantly that Jason gasped and had to shade his eyes from the glare.

What was it?

Then, suddenly, the light faded. The stone became plain grey once more and Jason's room was plunged into darkness. He went over to the window and pulled the curtains open, but heavy clouds covered the moon.

"I wonder if the stone reacts to moonlight?" he thought. He decided to ask Evie. Perhaps she could work it out.

Evie shuffled into his room, her eyes heavy with sleep. She didn't believe what had happened.

"Are you mad?" she grumbled. "Did you wake me up just to show me your stupid stone?"

Jason's eyes filled with tears. It was horrible not to be believed. But just then, as Evie turned to go back to her own room, the moon came out from behind the clouds, and the stone blazed into dazzling life again. Jason wrapped a handkerchief round it to dim its brilliance.

"Wow!" said Evie.

"It's weird. Magical!" said Jason, feeling uneasy. "I think we'd better put the stone back where we found it. It must belong to somebody, or something."

"How can we?" asked Evie. "We'd wake the whole neighbourhood with that bright light."

As they were standing there, thinking about what to do, something else quite extraordinary happened.

"Look at the moon, Evie!" cried Jason. "It's coming nearer!"

The huge, round shape of the moon suddenly filled the window. Enormous eyes seemed to stare at them, sweeping the room. It looked quite frightening, close up.

"It's got a face!" gasped Evie. "It looks as if it is searching for something!"

Jason knew just what to do. He picked up the stone and placed it on the windowsill. Then he opened the window. The Moon was terrifyingly close now. Its huge face seemed to absorb the light of the stone. As the children watched, the two flared into one bright light which dazzled them so much, they had to turn their faces away. When they looked back, the stone had disappeared.

As the light dimmed, they went to the window and looked out. The moon was back in its proper place in the night sky, but they could still make out its huge round face. And it was smiling!

CAT ON A BROOMSTICK

Life as a witch's cat was not exactly all Jetstone had hoped it would be.

When he had first arrived at Witch Humpledink's cottage, it all looked very promising. There was a roaring fire in the grate with a rug in front of it, where Jetstone settled himself comfortably. But as night fell, Witch Humpledink threw on her cloak and perched Jetstone on her broomstick.

How Jetstone hated that broomstick! How he hated those freezing night flights, with the wind chilling his very whiskers. Witch Humpledink never noticed the cold: the worse the weather, the more she seemed to enjoy herself.

Jetstone didn't dare complain in case she turned him into something horrid.

One particularly foul evening, when the rain was lashing against the cottage windows, Jetstone decided that he had had enough. "I don't want to be a witch's cat," he said. "I want a nice farmhouse kitchen, where I can catch mice during the day and sleep all night by the warm stove."

"Come, Jetstone!" called Witch Humpledink. "Time to go out."

Jetstone pretended not to hear.

"JETSTONE!" roared Witch Humpledink. "Come here AT ONCE!"

Jetstone reluctantly got to his feet and stretched, then followed the witch to the door. Witch Humpledink picked him up and deposited him on the broomstick. He clung on tight as it rose in the air and swooped giddily across to the wood.

Jetstone looked down at the wood passing beneath them with its carpet of soft leaves. It was now or never! He balanced precariously for a moment, and then he jumped.

It was a long way to the ground. But Jetstone landed the right way up, on all four feet – as cats do – and waited till the broomstick had flown out of sight. Then he ran through the wood until he came to a farmyard. He dived into the barn, shook off some of the rain and settled down to sleep in the dry hay.

"Look! A black cat!"

"Is it a stray?"

"He looks like Witch Humpledink's cat."

Jetstone opened his eyes to find the farmer, his wife and his little daughter all looking down at him.

"No, he can't be the witch's cat," said the wife. "Look – he has white whiskers. Witch Humpledink's cat is completely black."

White whiskers? Jetstone squinted down at them, and saw that they were indeed snowy white. He remembered jumping off the broomstick and running through the wood, terrified the witch would catch him. Perhaps his whiskers had turned white with fright. But whatever the reason, at least his days as a witch's cat were over: no self-respecting witch would want a black cat with white whiskers.

"Let's put him by the fire," said the farmer's wife. "He looks wet, cold and hungry."

Jetstone curled up in front of the warm kitchen stove, purring contentedly. He'd eaten a delicious bowl of meat scraps that the farmer's daughter had put before him, but best of all he'd taken his last broomstick ride!

DRAGON FIRE

At one time, dragons didn't breathe fire, so it was safe for them to live in houses.

Like all dragons, Clarence loved to be warm. He was happiest curled up and snoozing by a roaring fire in his cosy little house – but sometimes he just had to go out, and then he felt the cold.

One winter's day, Clarence was flying home when it started to snow. A snowflake plopped on to his nose.

"Brrr!" he shivered. "I wish I could carry my nice warm fire around with me, then I'd never feel cold again."

He was almost home but he thought his idea was such a good one that he turned and flew back to the cottage where the wizard lived.

"Hmm." The wizard frowned as Clarence explained what he wanted. "Fire spells can be dangerous, you know. They can get out of hand."

But Clarence pleaded so hard that the wizard finally took down his thick, leather-bound spell book and leafed through the pages.

"Ah, here we are," he said. He read the spell carefully, collected the ingredients and then stirred them into his big copper pot until they became a thick, green, horrible-smelling brew. The potion was ready.

"Open wide," said the wizard. Clarence swallowed the mixture. Ugh! It tasted vile. But suddenly he began to feel very hot. The spell must be working!

He thanked the wizard, and gave him five pieces of his precious dragon gold.

Outside in the snowy street, Clarence began to wonder if he'd parted with his gold a little too soon. There was no sign of fire around him that he could see. Although his insides were hot, the outside was as cold as ever, and he couldn't wait to get close to his fire.

As he turned the key to his front door, he felt a sneeze coming on. "Atish-atish-atishooooo! Oh, help!"

For as Clarence had opened his mouth to sneeze, a huge flame shot out of his mouth and scorched his lovely front door. He sneezed again as he went into the sitting room and this time he set fire to the curtains. In a very short time, Clarence's lovely little home had burnt to the ground! So much for carrying his fire around with him.

Clarence now had to find a new home that wouldn't catch fire every time he sneezed. He flew up into the hills and found a big, deep cave. He lit a bonfire in front of it, then wrapped himself in a flame-resistant blanket and fell fast asleep, snuggled down in the darkness.

As it turned out, Clarence was very pleased with his new home. His friends were impressed, too. They thought it was a very trendy place for a dragon – and very low-maintenance! Also, breathing fire was a jolly useful thing to be able to do.

One by one they all visited the wizard for their own fire spells. And that's how it was that dragons came to live in caves and breathe fire.

As for the wizard at the end of the lane, well he was happy. His fame spread far and wide and he became the most successful wizard in the land.

THE LITTLE YELLOW GOBLIN

Once upon a time, a little yellow goblin lived under a big stone in Nightingale Lane. He was an ugly fellow and fond of mean tricks. He would leap out and frighten a passing horse, so that it bolted with its rider. Or kick children on the ankle if they came near his stone. But no one ever saw him.

Except Jane. The goblin had just bitten Jane's friend, Betsy, on the leg. While Betsy hopped about, yelling, Jane looked around to see what had bitten her. She didn't have to look far: she spotted the small, wicked-looking, yellow goblin peeking from behind the stone.

"Hey, you!" cried Jane. "Why did you just bite my friend?"

The goblin tried to run away and hide, but Jane caught him by the scruff of the neck and held on tight as he struggled and squirmed.

"I asked you a question," she said.

"I know you did," said the goblin. "Let me go and I'll tell you."

"Oh, no," said Jane. "I know all about you and your tricks. I've a good mind to drop you in the village pond. It's very deep and very smelly."

"Please, no," squealed the goblin. "I can't swim."

"I'm sure Betsy – and all the other people you've hurt – wouldn't mind if you drowned, would you, Betsy?"

"I'd stamp on him, if I were you," said Betsy, rubbing her sore leg.

"Playing tricks is the only way I get noticed," muttered the goblin, sulkily. "I'm so small that no one ever sees me."

"You don't have to be nasty to be noticed!" said Jane. "Try being nice, instead!"

"But it's more fun being nasty."

"Yes, it is," agreed Jane. "Right, let's go to the pond!"

"All right!" cried the goblin, frantically. "I'll be nice, I promise."

"I bet he doesn't keep his promises," said Betsy.

"Goblin's word," said the goblin.

Jane let him go. "We'll know where to find you again if you don't," she warned.

Soon after, strange things started happening in Nightingale Lane. An old lady found a beautiful bunch of daffodils in her basket. And a lost traveller was helped on his way by a little yellow man, who took him to the nearest inn.

The next time that Jane and Betsy walked along Nightingale Lane they met a pleasant-faced young man – a little short perhaps – with a broad grin and sparkling eyes.

"You've grown!" said Jane in amazement, looking at the goblin that she'd last seen living under a stone.

"Every time I do a good deed, I grow a bit taller," said the goblin. "It feels very good."

"I'm glad to hear it," said Jane, as she shook his hand. "But don't stop being good once you've grown as tall as you want to be, will you?"

"I won't," said the goblin, grinning. "Goblin's word."

THE MONSTER IN THE POOL

In the middle of a dark wood was a deep and murky pool, and in the middle of the pool, there lived a monster. Everyone knew it was there. They'd seen its moon-eyes looking up at them in the water, or seen a scaly claw grasping at an overhanging branch. And everyone knew, too, that the monster ate people. It was said that the woodcutter's great-great-great grandfather had been gobbled up whole, and it was believed to be particularly fond of naughty children.

Most local people avoided the wood, knowing about the monster in the pool, but not Marcus Goodheart. He was a soldier travelling home on leave from the war and was looking forward to seeing his family again. He was anxious to get home as quickly as possible and cutting through the wood was the quickest way to his village.

He marched along at a brisk pace, singing as he went. He had seen so many horrors in battle, he wasn't bothered about a monster in a pool. In fact, he couldn't resist stopping by the pool to look into the brackish water. "It's just a silly tale," he thought. Then, deep down in the pool, something stirred.

Before Marcus could turn away, a huge shape lunged from the water and a wet, slimy hand grabbed his leg. He shook it, trying to break free, but then the rest of the monster emerged. It was very ugly, and a repulsive muddy-green colour.

"Let go of me!" demanded Marcus.

"No – please stay!" cried the monster.

"You can speak!" said Marcus, in amazement. It was polite, too!

The monster snorted loudly. "Of course I can," it said. "Not that I get much chance to practise. Nobody ever comes near me."

It let go of Marcus's leg and climbed out of the water and on to the bank.

"Well, I'm not surprised that no one comes near you," said Marcus, without thinking. "You're so …"

"I know," said the monster, dropping his head. "I'm ugly, that's why. All monsters are ugly. Otherwise they wouldn't be monsters." Tears dropped from his moon-eyes.

The monster had let go of Marcus's leg, but hadn't run away. Marcus could see that it was not an evil creature: just very lonely and sad.

"I expect you'd look very handsome to another monster," said Marcus. "But people are afraid because they think you will eat them."

"Eat them! Where did they get that idea? I'm a vegetarian. Always have been."

"What about the woodcutter's great-great-great grandfather …?"

"You don't think I'm that old, do you?" said the monster. "That was my great-great grandfather, the last carnivorous member of the family, and in any case the story has been grossly exaggerated. But we don't talk about him. I just want a bit of company and a chat."

Marcus reached out and patted the monster's large, clammy hand. "I'll come and see you," he promised. "And I'll bring my family, too, so that when I go back to my regiment you'll still have visitors."

The monster's moon-eyes glowed with gratitude.

The monster still lives in the pond in the middle of the wood, but now he has plenty of friends. The Goodhearts and the other villagers come to see him regularly. The pool has become a very popular place for picnics, and people always remember to bring extra fruit and vegetables for the monster, and especially his favourite strawberry buns.

ALL THAT GLITTERS

Barnaby Bassett and his wife, Mary, had a nice little cottage, and a fine black-and-white cow that gave them plenty of creamy milk. Yet despite their comfortable life, Barnaby was not happy. He wanted to be rich. He wished with all his heart that his cellar was full of gold.

"Even just one bag of gold would do," he said.

It's not that he wanted to spend it. He just wanted to be able to gloat over it. Barnaby Bassett had the makings of a true miser.

One evening, there was a knock on their door. Barnaby opened it and he saw a little man standing on the doorstep. He was dressed in green with a red feather in his cap.

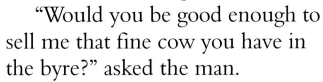

"Would you be good enough to sell me that fine cow you have in the byre?" asked the man.

"Sell her? But she's all we have," replied Barnaby.

"Don't even think of it," said Mary.

"She's a fine cow," said the man with a cunning look.

"Yes," said Barnaby, suddenly having an idea. "She's worth her weight in gold."

"And it's gold I'll be giving you," said the man, bringing a large, bulging sack from behind his back.

Barnaby licked his lips.

The little man took out a handful of shiny gold coins that glittered in the lamplight. He held one out to Barnaby, who took it with trembling fingers and bit it to make sure it was real.

"All right," said Barnaby quickly, before his wife could say anything. "The cow's yours."

"Don't come outside. It's a cold night," said the little man. "I'll lead her out myself."

He quickly disappeared into the darkness, leaving Barnaby with the sack.

"Give me a hand, Mary," he said. "This sack's very heavy."

Mary sighed. "I just hope you've done the right thing, I have a bad feeling about this. That little man looked like a leprechaun to me. You can't trust them, and you know how mischievous they can be."

She came over to the door and they each took hold of a corner of the sack and pulled. But to their amazement, it lifted easily and weighed nothing at all, as though it only contained featherdown.

With a sinking heart, Barnaby opened the sack. It was stuffed with leaves.

"B-but it was real gold, truly it was," he stammered.

"I told you!" said Mary, crossly. "But did you listen?"

They rushed to the window, but both the little man and the cow were gone.

"Perhaps now you'll stop dreaming of what you can't have and work for what you can," snapped Mary.

And from that day on, Barnaby worked hard until he had saved up enough money for another cow and no longer wasted time dreaming of a cellar full of gold.

NOT QUITE A DRAGON

Rachel and Patrick found the creature one day while they were walking home from school. Patrick went to throw an empty drink can into a litterbin, when he saw the rubbish move. He let out a cry of startled surprise.

"Rachel! There's something alive in here!"

They peered into the bin. Certainly, something was moving underneath some greasy chip paper. Suddenly, a head popped out, making the children jump.

They'd never seen anything like it. It had bulging amber eyes, a long tail and little spiky wings. Its greeny-yellow skin was scaly, like a lizard's. It wasn't very big – about the size of a small cat – and it was trying hard to scramble out of the bin.

"Wow! It looks like a dragon," said Patrick.

"A dragonet," said Rachel. "It's too small to be a dragon."

The dragonet gave a little chirp.

"It doesn't seem to want to be in the litter bin," said Patrick. "D'you think we ought to help it out?"

"Of course," said Rachel. She gripped the creature round the middle and hauled it out of the bin. It clung to her, its sharp claws catching in her sweater. She carefully unhooked them and it cuddled down in her arms.

Patrick gently stroked its scaly head with his finger.

"Can we take it home with us?" he asked. "Please, Rachel." But Rachel shook her head. She knew just how much Patrick wanted a pet, now that their old dog had died, but it wouldn't do to keep the dragonet.

"It would really be best to leave it on the pavement," she said. "It will probably make its own way home."

She put the dragonet down and she and Patrick walked away quickly. Unfortunately, the little thing seemed determined to follow them. It flapped its tiny wings and hopped awkwardly after them.

"Oh dear," said Rachel. "This isn't good —"

Just then they heard a tremendously loud wooshing noise overhead. They looked up to see a huge dragon soaring over them. Patrick yelped and ducked, but Rachel just stood and stared.

It was just like the dragonet, only bigger. It was the most amazing sight Rachel had ever seen. It swooped down and scooped up the tiny little creature on the pavement.

"Oh no!" said Patrick. "It will eat it!"

"No, it won't, stupid," said Rachel. "Can't you see? It's the little one's mother!"

Both children stared in wonder up at the sky, watching the amazing dragon with its huge wings fly away, until it was a spot in the far distance and finally vanished.

Rachel put her arm round her brother. "Don't be sad, Patrick. If we hadn't pulled the little dragon out of that litterbin, the mother would never have seen it. It would probably have starved to death."

"But I wanted to keep it," said Patrick, who was close to tears.

"We wouldn't have known what to feed it on," Rachel said sensibly. "It was best it went back to its mother."

And Patrick knew his sister was right.

WITCH TWINKLETOES

Witch Batswing was pulling on her long black boots one day, when she noticed the soles had huge holes in them. "Not even magic will put those right," she said. "I'll have to buy a new pair." And off she flew to the shoe shop in Witch Hollow.

The shop had a great many pairs of boots on display. Fine green leather boots, shiny red boots, and a black pair just like her own. But the ones that Witch Batswing fancied were silver and gold, sparkling with diamonds. They were dreadfully expensive. Witch Batswing hadn't nearly enough money in her purse for them, but a simple magic spell would put that right.

The other witches would hate them, of course: and the Chief Witch certainly didn't approve of showiness.

Despite her enormous feet and huge bunions, as soon as she put them on, the boots fitted Witch Batswing perfectly. They even made her feet look slim and elegant.

"I'll take them," she said, handing the shop assistant three gold pieces and telling him to keep the change.

The assistant beamed. "Oh, thank you, madam," he said, bowing. He was not so happy, though, after Witch Batswing had left the shop and he discovered the gold pieces had turned back into copper pennies.

That night people looked up and thought they saw a meteor shooting across the starry sky. It was shaped remarkably like a pair of boots. It came down near Spelltop Beacon, where the local witches held their coven.

"Well, what do you think of them?" said Witch Batswing, parading her new boots to her sister witches.

"Vulgar," said Witch Hemlock, enviously.

"TAKE THEM OFF!" screeched the Chief Witch. "No self-respecting witch would ever wear boots like those!"

"But they make me feel beautiful and elegant," said Witch Batswing, and it was true! She looked as radiant as a fairy princess. Her boots glittered and twinkled like a million stars. She was transformed.

Needless to say, she was immediately banished from the coven.

She became known as Witch Twinkletoes, famous for her herbal teas and healing potions.

Of course, she could never take off the magic boots. Without them she'd lose her good looks. Let's hope there's another pair exactly the same in the little shoe shop in Witch Hollow, for when the soles wear out!

THE WITCH AT THE BOTTOM OF THE LANE

Katie remembered first meeting the witch at the bottom of the lane when she was just three years old. She had stopped at the gate of a cottage to stroke a black cat and the witch had peered over the hedge at her. She had long, straggly hair and a set of yellow, sharp-looking teeth. Katie had been terrified, imagining the witch was going to eat her. Fortunately, her mum arrived at that moment and the witch disappeared into her cottage and shut the door.

As Katie grew older, she avoided that lane if she could, but never went past the witch's cottage without running. And she was never brave enough to stop and stroke the black cat.

Then one day, Katie and her mother were out shopping.

"Pop into the baker's, love, will you," said Mum, "and get us some chocolate cakes for tea."

There was a queue inside the shop. The baker's cakes were very popular. Katie waited her turn, until at last there was only one old lady in front of her.

"What can I get for you, Mrs Throgmorton?" asked the baker.

"One small brown loaf, please," said the old lady.

"I can't tempt you into buying one of my chocolate cakes?" joked the baker.

"I'd love to, but I can't afford it," said Mrs Throgmorton.

Katie felt dreadful. Fancy not being able to afford one cake!

"That's awful!" said Mum, when Katie told her about the old lady. "Pop back inside and get two more for Mrs Throgmorton."

Katie ran back to the baker's shop which was still very busy and by the time she had bought the extra cakes, the old lady was almost out of sight.

Katie and her mother called to her, but she seemed to be hard of hearing, so they hurried after her in time to see her turn into the lane where the witch lived!

"Oh, no," said Katie. "Must we go down there? I really don't want to go past the witch's house," she pleaded.

"Don't be silly, Katie," said Mum. "You're far too old now to still believe in witches."

Katie was nearly eight, but she could still remember how frightened she had been all those years ago, when the witch had peered at her over the hedge. She held on tightly to her mother's hand.

"Mrs Throgmorton!" called Katie's mum, and the old lady turned her head.

To Katie's horror, the old lady was opening the gate to the witch's garden. "That's the witch's house!" Katie said to her. "Don't go in!"

"It's where I live," said Mrs Throgmorton. "Always have and always will."

Mum gave Mrs Throgmorton the cakes and the old lady smiled with pleasure. Her face was kind and her smile was warm. How could Katie have thought so badly of her?

"You can imagine the silliest things when you're very young," thought Katie, feeling ashamed. "She's just a lonely old lady. I expect she'd like me to visit her." And Katie did visit, every Monday after school, and always took a bag of special cakes.